Walt Disney
PICTURES PRESENTS

Lilo & Stitch 2

Stitch Has A Glitch

Adapted by Frank Berrios
Illustrated by Sean Sullivan

A Random House PICTUREBACK® Book
Random House New York

Library of Congress Control Number: 2004117489   ISBN: 0-7364-2334-6

www.randomhouse.com/kids/disney

Printed in the United States of America   10 9 8 7 6 5 4 3 2 1

"A-lo-ha!" Stitch rocketed his spaceship toward a crowded beach. The little alien laughed as screaming humans ran away in fear. After creating a stampede, Stitch was ready to cause more damage on the island. Suddenly, from far off, he heard a voice—

"Stitch, wake up!" cried Lilo.

"It's okay. You were just having another nightmare," explained Lilo. Lilo listened as Stitch described his dream. "It's my professional opinion that you are afraid of turning bad again," she said. Then Lilo showed Stitch that he had nothing to worry about because his goodness level was extra high.

Later that day, Lilo learned that her hula class would participate in the town's hula contest. All the girls were excited about working on costumes with their mothers—except Lilo.

"I guess Lilo's on her own," said Mertle. "She doesn't have a mom."

Kumu could see that Lilo was hurt. So he gave Lilo a special picture of her mother, who had won the same hula contest when she was Lilo's age.

Lilo loved the photo of her mother, but she didn't think she'd be able to win the contest. "My mom was beautiful like an orchid and graceful like a wave. I'll never be like her," she said.

But Stitch believed in Lilo. He convinced her that if they worked together, she could win.

That night at home, something weird happened to Stitch—
his eyes began to glow and he made a big mess. Everyone
thought he was being naughty except Jumba.

"I hoped this day would never come," said Jumba
mysteriously as he raced to his lab. Pleakley followed him.

In the lab, Jumba told Pleakley about the day he had created Stitch. Something had gone terribly wrong. The intergalactic police had burst in and arrested Jumba before he could finish charging Stitch!

"Now his circuits are going haywire," Jumba explained, "and if it continues, they will burn themselves out like supernova." Jumba had to figure out a way to save Stitch before he shut down — forever!

Before long, Jumba had some good news. "I finished plans for a new fusion chamber that will recharge Stitch," he said. "However, we don't have alien technology to build it. We must find primitive Earth machinery and just hope it works."

So Pleakley was sent out on a secret mission to collect the items they needed.

During practice for the hula contest, Stitch's eyes began to glow
again. "Stitch, what are you doing? Cut it out!" yelled Lilo. But Stitch
could not control himself. He growled and threw things at the other
girls, sending them screaming out of the classroom.

Lilo was mad at Stitch for ruining hula practice. Stitch wanted to prove to her that he wasn't really bad, so he did lots of good deeds. He fed worms to a hungry baby bird and helped an old lady cross the street.

"I'm all good now, no more badness," Stitch said.

But that night, without warning, Stitch began to lose control again. In a wild fit, he accidentally destroyed Lilo's room—and the costume she had made for the big contest! Afterward, Stitch tried to explain that there was something wrong with him. But Lilo had her own opinion. "You're bad, and you'll always be bad," she told Stitch.

Lilo was really upset.

"I have to win the contest, just like Mom did," she told her older sister, Nani. "If I win, she'll know I'm good and she'll be proud of me."

"I think Mom would be proud of you just for being you," replied Nani.

The next day at the contest, just as Lilo was about to go onstage, Stitch felt the badness coming on again. And as his body began to shake, he accidentally scratched Lilo!

Stitch thought he was becoming dangerous, as he had been in his nightmare, so he tried to leave Earth on Jumba's spaceship. When Stitch ran away, Lilo finally understood that something must be wrong with him. He would never hurt her on purpose.

Although she really wanted to win, Lilo left the contest to help her friend.

"Stitch is in trouble," she said as she ran off. "He needs me." Jumba, Pleakley, Nani, and her boyfriend, David, followed.

Lilo and the others soon found Stitch, but he didn't look good.
"Get him into the fusion chamber before his energy runs out!"
said Jumba.

"Stitch, you're gonna be okay now," said Lilo. "Please be okay." But Stitch looked even worse than before.

Jumba checked the energy level on the machine and gave them the bad news: "We're too late."

Lilo took Stitch in her arms. "You're my *'ohana*, Stitch, and I'll always love you," she said.

Suddenly, the energy levels on Jumba's machine began to rise, and Stitch was fully charged. He was okay!

"Stitch better?" asked Stitch.

Lilo smiled. "No more nightmares."

"You had us all worried," said Pleakley. "Group hugs! Jumba, c'mon, it's a touching moment, literally."

Later that night, the entire family joined Lilo and Stitch onstage as they performed their special hula dance.

"Mom would be so proud of you," said Nani.

Lilo knew her sister was right—and that their mom was looking down on them and smiling.